MW00353868

SCHMUCK THE BUCK

Santa's Jewish Reindeer

BOOKS

NYC · USA · EARTH

Schmuck the Buck Copyright © 2018 EXO Books, LLC.
A work of fiction. All rights reserved.

Poetry consulting by Jared Harél

Library of Congress Control Number: 2018953653
ISBN 978-0-9975902-7-2 (Hardcover)
ISBN 978-0-9975902-9-6 (Paperback)

www.EXOBooks.com

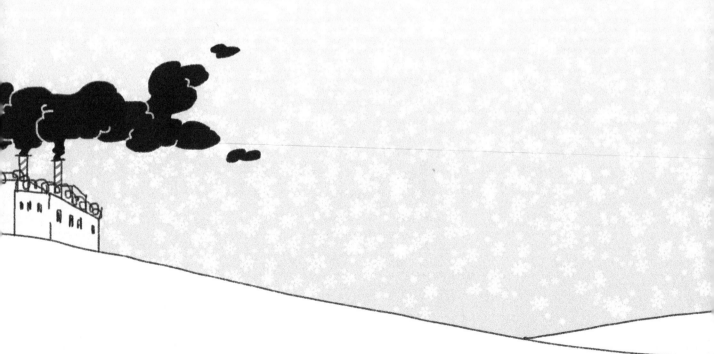

karina Shor
2018

WRITTEN BY EXO BOOKS
ILLUSTRATED BY KARINA SHOR

Now you probably know about Santa's other reindeer.
That's okay—we're not telling that old story here.
So forget Dasher and Dancer and Prancer and Vixen
And Comet and Stupid and Donder and Blitzen.
And screw Rudolph, the hero for the last 79 years,
Always leading the pack to thunderous cheers.

Our tale is about another, somewhat down on his luck,
It's about Santa's Jewish reindeer, Schmuck the Buck.

When we look back into younger Schmuck's life,
We see long days filled with hardship and strife.
Because to a shy, awkward buck named Larry
Reindeer Junior High always seemed kinda scary.

You see, Larry was just your average caribou
Who liked to eat grass and chew and chew and chew.
But growing up average was still pretty cruel,
As Larry found out from an older buck at school.

The other young reindeer were playing a game
But every so often, out rang a name.
The bully kept calling Larry a schmuck!
From then on, the name Schmuck just stuck.

Teen Schmuck tried out for the
JV sled squad,
But slipped and suffered a badly
sprained quad.

Teen Schmuck asked a cute doe to the dance,
The doe just laughed, and sneered, "Not a chance!"

Now, there weren't many jobs in the North Pole area,
The brutally harsh winters being the primary barrier.
So young Schmuck made the pragmatic decision
To aspire towards a well-paying managerial position.
He studied very hard and got straight A's in school,
Earning a B.S. in Accounting with a concentration in Yule.

Factories of elves slaved long hours building toys,
For hundreds of millions of little girls and boys.
They worked every day and toiled through the nights,
Filling Santa's warehouses with wondrous delights.

That December, Hanukkah began on a Sunday,
Which didn't affect operations in any way.
Someone still needed to make all the gifts,
So Santa had everyone work nineteen-hour shifts.

Yet Schmuck, true to form, had been coming in early,
And requested time off from the HR doe, Shirley.

Schmuck left work at three to be with his kin,
Happily skipping away from the company din.

He pranced his way through the piney flora,
Racing home just in time to light the Menorah.

Dinner was at Schmuck's family's stable,
Mother, Father, Aunt and Uncle sat 'round the table.
His Mother's grass latkes were famously delish,
A nice (Jewish) doe for her son her number one wish.

Larry, he arrived at the peak of the hype-
The family was calling Bubby Rose in Boca on Skype.

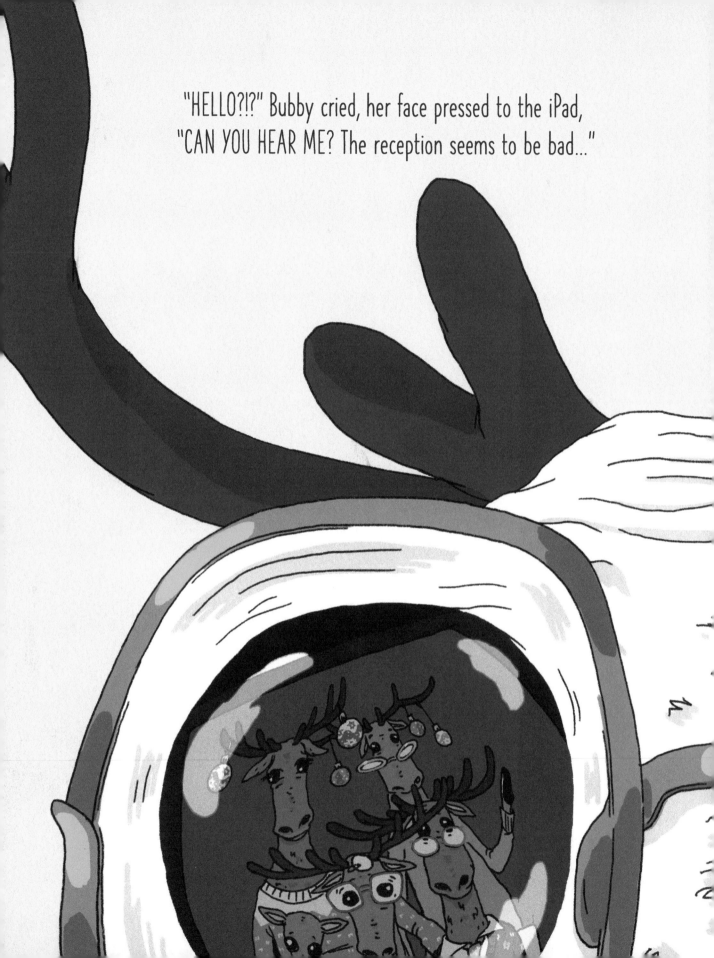

"HELLO?!?" Bubby cried, her face pressed to the iPad,
"CAN YOU HEAR ME? The reception seems to be bad..."

Schmuck left work early for the
next seven days,
Quality time during the holidays
(but of course at no pay).

HANGIN' OUT WITH
THE HOMIES...

NEW HANUKKAH SWAG!
THANX BUBBY! ♥

He visited with friends, and ate yummy food,
Taking time to enjoy the holiday mood.

But of course, some co-workers started to grumble,
And this time of year is no time to stumble.
So Schmuck vowed to work harder after his holiday away,
Including a forty-eight hour shift Christmas Eve into Christmas Day.

Giving gifts to others is an expression of cheer
It's a massive operation getting bigger each year.
Christmas Eve is stressful in every imaginable way,
Packing billions of toys into Santa's one sleigh!

But here's a secret you'll learn right now in this story:
Santa's deliveries don't always go hunky-dory.
Things go awry, like a mislabeled gift,
Or that time it was foggy and Rudolph provided the lift.

Yet this year, the screw-up was even bigger than most,
Affecting kids from the East to West Coast.
The worst of the blunder was it was no longer night,
Santa and his crew already back from their flight!
Schmuck was at his desk, when to his surprise,
'Twas a sight to be seen with his own very eyes!

His big boss Aisha comes huffing in a hurry,
Filled with worry and cursing up a flurry.
"Just think how the little girls and boys will be shaken,
When their new toys don't have batteries when they awaken!

Nine warehouses were found still filled with batteries,
Single C's, double A's, triple A's, multiple D's!
Some stupid dummies forgot to load up the toys,
Nothing will light up – No fun! No noise!
This is one giant elfin' disaster –
We have no choice but to wake up the master!"

Now here is another fact that you'll learn:
Santa has very particular orders on his return.
And one thing that would spell certain doom
Was disturbing Mr. & Mrs. Claus before noon!

"But wait!" said Schmuck from the back of the place,
"Waking up Santa would be a disgrace!
There's an answer to this problem, I'll tell you how,
The only thing is, we need to do it right now.
Let's send a mass text to all the kids' parents,
All aunts and uncles and of course the grandparents."

So sorry, but unfortunately this year batteries aren't included. Walmart's open though.

"Are you crazy!?" cried Aisha, "That kills the whole dream!
The elves, us reindeer, this whole North Pole scheme.
Our whole reputation is rooted in magical thought.
A mass text will leave the whole world distraught!"

"Don't worry," Schmuck said, "a text will be fine,
The last thing they want is to hear their kids whine.
The adults will do this no problem, you'll see,
As long as our labors are under that tree!
We already have all their information in our database,
So I urge you to reconsider for this special case."

"Okay, Schmuck...," Aisha allowed with a frown,
"But if this goes south, know that it will go down
That texting half the planet was YOUR idea,
Santa will know,
After which he'll probably kick your butt to
the snow!"

Schmuck took the utmost of care,
But executing the plan was a simple affair.

He composed the mass text just like he said,
Then hit send with a confident nod of his head.

"That's it," said Schmuck after a series of shrugs.
"That's it!" erupted the elves, giving each other hugs.

"We'll see..." said Aisha with a grimace on her face.
"We'll see..." as silence descended on the place.

You could hear Santa's T.V. on inside his house,
But outside, the North Pole was silent as a mouse.

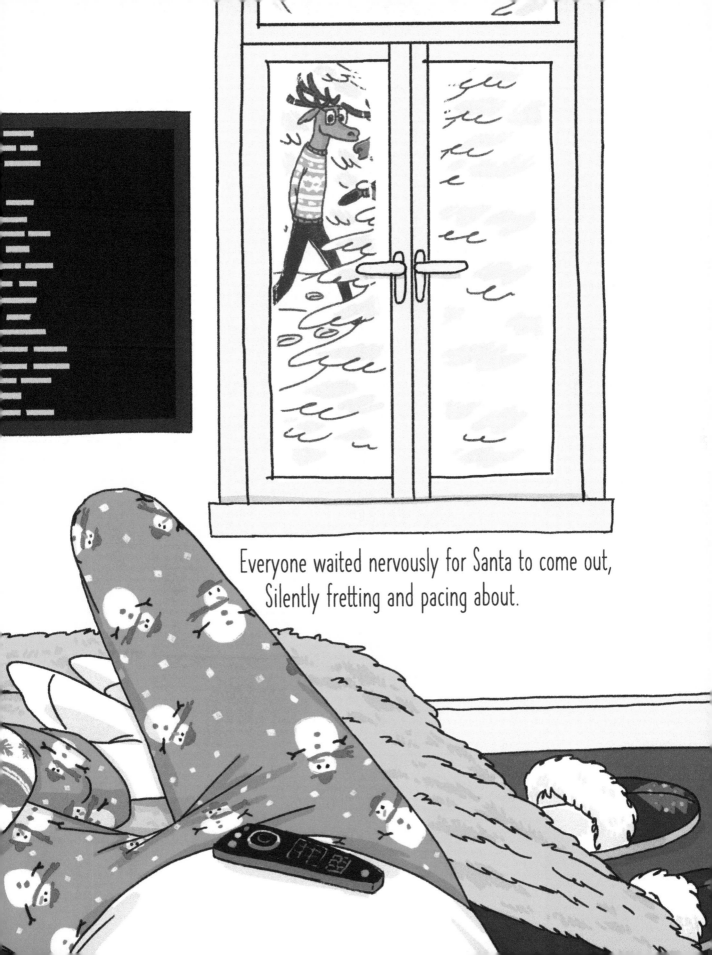

Everyone waited nervously for Santa to come out,
Silently fretting and pacing about.

At 1:38 PM the front door opened up,
And out came Santa Claus, egg nog in his cup.

"Good Christmas, guys!" he said, then let out his laugh,
Warming the hearts of the whole North Pole staff.
"Seriously, guys-good move with that mass text.
Whoever thought of it gets to sit with me next."

Now the fellow they had always called names
And no longer allowed in their games
Was the envy of all, or at least around here,
For no greater honor can grace a reindeer.

The bucks felt sorry that they'd ever been mean
When Santa said, "Well Schmucky, I've never seen
A reindeer more resourceful than you.
And I thought Vixen knew a thing or two!"

The growing crowd applauded before starting to scream,
"Hurray for Larry!" "Larry, speak to the team!"
Our hero blushed and looked around with a grin
That nearly connected his ears with his chin!

Schmuck said, "We have our differences, that's for sure,
But we're all the same at the core.

Christmas isn't just about gifts, but the love underneath,
So it really doesn't matter your religious belief.
We give because we care, we love, and want to please,
So there's room for every one of us under our Christmas trees."

Now the same reindeer who used to tease him
Would do anything in the world just to please him.

Larry now rode with Santa in the back of the sleigh.
Schmuck was a pimp daddy. Go, Larry. Hurray!

EXO Books is the pen name and publishing company
of a man from NYC, USA, Earth.
This is his second book.
Find out more at EXOBooks.com

Karina Shor is the alter ego of an artist and
illustrator from Israel currently living in Brooklyn.
Her savvy cheekiness is embodied in many works.
See more at KarinaShor.com

HAPPY HOLIDAYS!

CPSIA information can be obtained
at www.ICGtesting.com
Printed in the USA
BVHW02*0103090918
526656BV00002B/3/P

9 780997 590272